Praise for Bad God's Tower:

"A nod to *No Country for Old Men* or Stephen King's *The Gunslinger*, Immersive setting, terrifyingly relatable characters, and unflinching horror coalesce in this fast-paced read."

- Mia Faller, Author of *Buried Women Speak*

***

"Engrossing from start to finish. This deserves 5 stars. This western elements are superb and the horror is blended so fluidly that the plot left me wanting to read everything this author has written. I've already bought some of her other novellas and can't wait to read them given how much I enjoyed this!"

- Brendon James, *Indie Horror Reviews*

***

"This story is a horror fan's dream. It's *Funny Games* meets T*he Descent* in the old west. What more could you ask for?" -*Chisto Healy, Author of Two of a Kind and the Bucket List*

***

"Bad God's Tower is a powerhouse of story-telling, packing in story and character, in a genre piece that pulls no punches in the *western,* or the *horror*. Building to a shocking conclusion, the story wends across the open landscape with a cast of characters, made only more colourful by blood. I loved it! I can't wait to see more from Erica Summers."

- Ash Ericmore, Author of *The Red Room* and *Our Skin of Deadwood*

***

"What starts off as a straightforward shoot-em-up western, morphs into a chaotic, cosmic, beasty rampage! This one will have you wiping the dust from your eyes and reloading your six-shooter when all is said and done!"

- Steve Stred, 2-time Splatterpunk Nominated author of *Mastodon*, *Father of Lies: The Complete Series*, and *Churn the Soil*

***

"*Bad God's Tower* is Erica Summers at her most ferocious in terms of deft storytelling. It features oppressive claustrophobia and is loaded with action-packed chaos and grisly horror. Summers is a writer to keep an eye on!"

- Otis Bateman, author of *Maggot Girl*

***

"…I'm looking forward to reading a lot more from Summers in the future. I wouldn't be surprised if I see this as a movie on Netflix someday. 5 big, shiny, sheriff stars!"

- Leeanne Wright, Reviewer

***

"A fast-paced, violent ride from start to finish. The ending will have you literally gasping for breath. Bad God's Tower is a book you can read in a single sitting and one I highly recommend."

-John Watson, *Author & Reviewer*

BAD GOD'S TOWER

A Western Horror Novelette

By

Erica Summers

BAD GOD'S TOWER

Edited by Amanda Jean Ruzsa

Proofread by Mark Anthony

Cover by Christy Aldridge of Grim Poppy Designs

Stay tuned at the end of the book for a full chapter sneak peek of the upcoming novel *Vanity Kills,* out September 1, 2023 in ebook, paperback, and hardcover editions.

MORE BY ERICA SUMMERS

Novellas & Novels

Bad God's Tower

Mantis

Vanity Kills

Published Short Stories:

"Take a Breath" (HellBound's *Anthology of Splatterpunk)*

"Tines" (Eerie River's *It Calls From Below)*

"*The Mother*" (Dark Lake's *Their Ghoulish Reputation)*

"Painted in Vermilion" (Eerie River's *Air: Elemental*

Series)

"All the Same Color on the Inside" (Year Five Anthology)

"In the Blood of the Martyr" (Amazon Kindle Unlimited)

DEDICATIONS

For Heather:

My muse. My spit-balling idea-woman. My peer. My problem-solver. My ARC reader. My sister. My soulmate. My she-ro.

For Dave, the absolute love of my life.

Thank you for believing in me.

Special thanks to my ARC team: *Ash Ericmore, Otis Bateman, Steve Stred, Chisto Healy, Mia Faller, Mark Anthony, John Ryland, & Leeanne Wright*

TRIGGER WARNINGS

Gore & Violence

Profanity

Abuse

Death

Death of an Animal (brief)

Period racism (mild)

"Traveling together on this ol' filly,

Sharing the stars, souls tied as one,

Ride any trail, the night is ours"

- Paul Cauthen, *Saddle*

"True cowboys are the ones who aren't afraid to get

dirty."

- Lane Frost, *American Rodeo Cowboy*

CHAPTER ONE

"**H**elp!" Chester hollered, his voice steeped in true terror. "Officer Montgomery, he's hurtin' bad!" He smashed his pasty white face between the iron bars. "Please! Don't let 'em die. He's 'closest ta' family I got!"

Brand new to the job, an apprehensive guard approached the frantic, tow-headed inmate with trepidation, unsure of protocol for the situation. A salty well rose in Chester Craven's arresting green eyes. Spit dribbled from his foul-smelling mouth. His teeth, the sparse few that remained, were the color of dry soil and his panicked lungfuls of spent breath reeked as if his organs were rotting inside him.

Eugene roared out painfully from the corner of the cage. He clutched his gut and his hulking body thrashed about the lower bunk.

"Please, Montgomery! He needs a doctor! Somethin's real wrong!" Chester's drawl advertised his severe lack of education. He pulled his face tight to the iron shafts again. "He's not long for this world if someone don't help 'im soon!"

Montgomery peered in at the source of the agonizing commotion. His voice cracked but he quickly regained composure. "Dempsey, what's wrong with you?"

Eugene didn't respond, but howled out again.

Chester bounced around the concrete floor like a rubber ball. "I just told ya, he's sick!"

"I want it from the horse's mouth!" Montgomery barked, his voice drenched in fear.

The distressed prisoner wailed louder. Chester retreated and rubbed tears from his cheeks, smearing trails of dirt on his filthy face.

Eugene was a true *beast* of a man. He had huge fists with tough knuckles marred from correcting jokes about his noticeable hair-lip scar throughout the years. The deformity he'd had since birth tore the center of his top lip up into a point like draped theater curtains. The rest of his bristly face was sun-damaged, awash with the tint of tanned rawhide.

But what Montgomery, a jailer of less-than-average height, found most intimidating was Eugene's gargantuan, almost inhuman, stature. He didn't want to go anywhere near the convict. To approach a man like Eugene Dempsey in this much agony seemed akin to hugging a wounded grizzly.

Chester's voice grew more frantic. "You just gon' let 'im *die*?! 'Er's a special place in Hell for cowards like you!"

Montgomery knew the idiot was right. It was his duty to act. "Against the wall, Craven!" The guard motioned to the far end of the cell and grabbed the heavy ring of keys from his belt. Chester followed the order with complete obedience. Eugene screamed in torment, whipping his broad body against the covers of his cot.

Montgomery unlocked the iron door and approached with caution, splitting his attention between Eugene and Chester like a pendulum.

"Think you can walk, Dempsey?" Montgomery stared into Eugene's black eyes, like those of a feral animal. "Or-"

Montgomery's words stopped short. Chester wrenched the jailer's biceps backward in a fluid motion. Eugene's massive hands drove a hunk of whittled wooden toothbrush up into Montgomery's belly like lightning flashes striking in quick succession.

Chester released the jailer's uniformed arms and jumped around like an excited monkey in the zoo, unable to contain thrilled screeches. The expression of betrayal never faded from Montgomery's face, even as Eugene jammed the wood spike into the guard's fleshy throat, twice, for good measure. The traumatic impact of the weapon opened the man's jugular like a steam-pipe atop a railway train.

Montgomery's blood spurted across Eugene's striped prisoner's uniform, staining the horizontal lines in warm, viscous vital fluids. Beneath his brawny chest, Eugene's heart thundered with adrenaline as he yanked it out and positioned it lower, burying the sharpened end into the guard's guts and torso with a powerful barrage of rapid-fire stabs. Chester ricocheted around the cell with boundless energy, cheering jovially at the top of his lungs.

Eugene threatened his cellmate with a piercing glare. Chester reeled himself in. After spending months in a tiny room with the man, he knew what the burly inmate was capable of, and those things -- in addition to the man's sheer size -- sent a burst of ice rushing through his veins.

The hall was corpse-quiet now. Eugene unclasped his giant mitt from the sharpened shaft of the toothbrush handle embedded between two of Montgomery's ribs, letting the wounded guard slump to the blood-soaked floor. Montgomery wormed his shuddering frame toward the open stall door, toothbrush still buried in his innards.

Chester yanked the boots from Montgomery's dragging feet and clumsily tugged them onto his own. "Hope ya' don't mind if we borrow these." Chester reared back and kicked him hard in the chest with every bit of brutal force the boot could afford him. Montgomery gurgled through a mouth full of blood at the barbaric impact. Chester's laugh echoed around the cell block. He always reminded Eugene of a hyena: perpetually in hysterics. "Oooh, I like the toe on 'ese!"

"Is it done?" The voice arose like a faint wisp of smoke from several cells down. It was Akecheta, whose name meant "fighter" in Sioux, which Eugene found ironic since the old man had exhibited nothing but a peaceful presence in his weeks at the Wyoming Territorial Prison. If not for the Lakota, he would have had no aspirations to orchestrate such a grisly murder. Nor would he have been called to action by a sudden, searing desire for the sweet taste of freedom and unfathomable wealth.

Chester cackled and mopped his snot up with his filthy forearm. "Yeah, i's done. Eugene done jus' stuck 'is ol' feller's spoon to the wall!" He grabbed the crotch of his banded black-and-white pajamas and seized joyfully, giggling like a child. "Go on! Climb 'at golden staircase, ya' greasy turnkey!"

Eugene wiped his soaked, bear-sized paws across his striped top, snatched up the fallen key ring, and stepped over the fading man.

Once to the hallway, Eugene hooked a left and started to unlock Akecheta's door. It felt bizarre to finally put a face to the voice. Akecheta had only arrived a short time ago, but they had talked at great length every night. Eugene considered him a friend despite never having laid eyes upon the man's face, until now. What a memorable face it was...

The Lakota man placed a mutilated hand in front of the keyhole to block it. "No, I want to stay." The man took a gulp of air and caressed the comforting vertical bars between them. His hands were gnarled and scarred by dozens of perfectly spaced indentations as though he'd been skewered by an entire box of nails. His face peeked out from behind a curtain of straight, white hair and his bronze skin was blanketed in strange chemical burns.

"After what I've seen..." The waver of his voice made Eugene uneasy. "It's safer here." Terror glossed over the grotesque man's bourbon-colored eyes, and he limped back to his bunk. His tranquil voice declared, "*May Wakan Tanka* protect you."

"I won't forget this." Eugene held up a folded piece of dingy paper with gratitude.

"No." Akecheta stared off into the middle of his enclosure in horror. "I don't imagine you will."

"C'mon, Eugene! Let's *git*!" Chester shouted.

Eugene raced back toward the claustrophobic cell they'd been imprisoned in for years and tossed the ring to Chester. He knelt inches beyond the bars and leered at the dying man as his scrawny cellmate twisted the key in the lock, sealing in the hemorrhaging guard. He spoke again to Montgomery who had paled from a fatal amount of blood loss.

"Who's the prisoner *now*?" Eugene grinned.

CHAPTER TWO

Walter waved a finger at the bartender who poured a glass of precisely what he wanted: the usual double of the Black Hills Saloon's finest bourbon, neat. Fine liquor was a luxury he enjoyed as an occasional treat since his nerve-wracking emancipation decades prior. He now equated the flavor on his tongue with the hard-earned sense of freedom.

He waved two fingers at the barkeep and, once served, slid the second glass of pricey spirits down to the private at his right, a trainee by the name of

George Fisher whom he had taken under his wing. The intoxicated soldier stared at a yellowed slip of paper with barely legible writing.

Walter Brown clung to his service rank as a Corporal. Everyone who had been part of his life before the war was gone now, including the love of his life. Hanna had been unfortunate enough to die at the hands of their owner in the servitude she'd been born into, never having experienced real freedom. Thoughts of her final moments plagued him sometimes, but he imagined how proud she would've been to witness him victorious in the Civil War, and later, his rise in the ranks to a Buffalo Soldier in the North. Memories of her awe-filled brown eyes and soft, angelic voice brought a slight smile to his aging face.

"Hear about this, suh'? Reward," George read the Western Union telegraph aloud, "five hunned dolla's each for the arrest of fu....fugitives Eugene Dempsy and Ch...ester Craven." Though he still struggled some, learning to read had become a source of pride for him over the last decade. "Oooh-wee!

That's a lotta greenbacks, suh'," George continued. "Said deys busted out da Wyomin' Ter... terri... territorial Prison. Bof' white men."

Walter scoffed. *Of course.*

"Woah. Says Dempsey be almost sev'n feet *tall.* Can't be right." He elbowed Walter, chuckling. "Whatchu even say ta' a man 'dat huge? *Stop... please*?" He burst into full-on laughter, slamming his coffee-colored fist down against the wooden bar top in a quick burst of noise.

"Wouldn't say nothin.'" Walter paused. "I'd let ma' carbine do the talkin'." He wasn't amused. It was bad enough they often found themselves ambushed, dodging silent Sioux arrows. The thought of tangling with a seven-foot white escapee and his idiot accomplice, Sharps carbine in tow or not, made his whirling brain anxious.

"Wouldn't even know what ta' do wit' all 'dat bounty money." Fisher's mind leaped around multiple outrageous expenses before changing the subject. "You reckon they's comin' up dis way?"

"Nope. Got no bidness trekkin' all 'da way up here. Disregard, soldier."

"Whateva' you say, boss." George stuffed the telegraph in the pocket of his flannel shirt and bounced his eyebrows flirtatiously at an attractive woman sitting across the saloon in his eyeline. She grinned coyly and then a large man quickly sat down beside her. He locked eyes with George, as if to say, "I see you eyein' my woman, *boy*."

Walter watched the interaction and mumbled into his glass. "Playin' wit' fire. You's too much balls, not enough brains, boy." He sipped the last settled bit of liquor from the glass. "We gon' work on that."

Walter slid from his stool and forked over two bits, enough to cover his tab, which was a large -- but worthwhile -- chunk of his thirteen-dollar-a-month salary. He pinched the bill of his gray-brown kepi and tipped the hat respectfully at the staff.

He shuffled backward and straightened his dark blue blouse. "Turnin' in, Fisha'. You stayin'?"

George nodded and lifted a shot glass to cheer his superior. "Feelin' liberated! Night's young!" Fisher downed the liquid, tugged at his corn-colored neckerchief and then drummed energetically on the counter.

"Don't drink too much, Fisha'. 'At's an orda'." Walter smoothed the wrinkles at his hips with his hands and brushed past his trainee. "You start laggin' tomorra', I'mma make you regret every drop." He chuckled softly. "I'll make ya' clean 'da horse barracks."

Fisher winced, then offered a respectful nod to the corporal. "Whateva' you say, boss."

CHAPTER THREE

A smoldering rage surged behind Eugene's irises. The rancher and his wife had fought harder than he'd anticipated. The tiny confines of his cell hadn't done the muscles he'd amassed on the railroad any favors either. Eugene could taste his own blood on his cleft lip where the woman had attacked him with a frying pan to the face. She'd only nicked him in the mouth with her wild flailing, but it still hurt like hell.

They were bound now, tied to the chairs at their own dinner table. Rancher and wife. *Oscar and Lena.* They'd cried each other's names out at the start of the home invasion. The criminals had taken note.

"This loaded, Oscar?" Eugene asked. He stared up at the rancher's pristine shotgun, mounted above the hearth, with immense curiosity. It was a chestnut brown Winchester 1873, like the one he had prior to incarceration; it was identical all the way down to the rich hue of the stock. He plucked it from the wall mount and held it like a newborn, caressing the side plate with his enormous thumb.

Chester slapped Oscar hard in the face. Lena began to bawl. "C'mon then! The man asked ya' a question. It's rude not ta' answer!"

Oscar huffed through gritted teeth and shook his head. Chester held a hand to his ear to imply he couldn't hear him.

"No!" He growled. "I don't keep it loaded."

"See?" Chester giggled. "That wasn't so bad!"

Eugene placed the butt of the weapon against his shoulder, raised the barrel, and peered down the sights at Lena's face. The rancher and his wife flinched. Lena let out an intense blubber of grievous sounds and whipped her head away.

Chester tugged at the seat of his oversized pants. Moments before, he and Eugene had rifled through the couple's belongings and ditched their striped prison duds for tattered, ill-fitting ranch wear. Eugene's new cowboy boots were tight enough to be a second skin and Chester's twiggy frame was swallowed by enough excess fabric for an additional outfit, but beggars couldn't be choosers.

After all, *it was only for a few days.*

"Ya' see... back there, at the door... see, we didn't wanna hafta' do no jiggery-pokery, but we knew ya' wouldn't open up if we was wearin' striped pajamas. We had no choice but ta' trick ya'." Chester cracked himself up. Between bursts of laughter, he spoke, "I can't believe two naked fellers stroll up to yer' door... an' you jus'... let 'em in!"

Chester Craven was a live wire, with a hyena's laugh, on a constant quest for chaos. He was a lean ball of energy wrapped in a sallow, malnourished body and punctuated with a deep set of shockingly-colorful irises. His eyes were the color of ripe pears, offset by thick, dark rings, like some sort of scraggly sleep-devoid lemur. Sprigs of wispy, blonde hair peppered his head and Lena thought the sickening intruder seemed like some kind of ghastly demon.

"We tried to help you," rang Lena's voice, furious through her tears. "Please let us go! We're nice people. We mind our own."

"Ain't no such thang as *good people*," Chester uttered with a foul, wide grin.

Eugene held up a thick hand to quiet his cohort. Chester was wise enough to pipe down, a feat not easy for him. He chewed his tongue to keep from talking, a habit he'd picked up from his uncle as a child.

"You got a pickaxe, friend?"

Oscar wanted to laugh at the brawny madman calling him *friend* but begrudgingly nodded instead.

"Where?" Eugene's patience was thin. His tone was downright demonic. Every time he spoke, his baritone voice drew attention and commanded respect.

"Just please, let us go and I'll show you where it's at," Oscar pleaded. "You can have anything you want. Food, money, horses… we won't stand in your way one bit." His shaking voice sounded sincere in between his heavy, panting breaths.

Without another word, Eugene activated the lower lever of the Winchester and fired the shotgun at Oscar's head. The thunderous blast ripped an instant hole through the man's face, blowing shattered fragments of skull into the air like a detonated firework. Lena screeched, sprayed with slick bits of viscera and hunks of hairy scalp. A glob of gray brain-matter dripped down the side of her face. She bled, too, from the handful of stray pellets that instantly burrowed deep into her flesh just from the proximity.

The tone of Lena's scream was horrific, and guttural, below the intense high-pitched ringing from the blast.

Chester cackled loudly, slapping his knee at the comical brutality.

"Wasn't what I asked," Eugene croaked at the body, eerily calm.

"What have you done?!" Flooded by absolute despair, Lena's throat tore with each screamed word.

Chester roared with surprised laughter and squatted before the remainder of the rancher's corpse.

"Had my doubts, but you still got it, Eugene!" Chester howled. "Hot *damn*, what a mess!" Still near the gnarled heap, he giggled up at Lena. His southern drawl was thick. "Looks like yer husband here was a liar."

Eugene grabbed a sack from the kitchen and dumped out the potatoes, scattering them on the floor. In their place, he stuffed the burlap with food and bottles of hooch. He rifled through drawers and emptied some ammunition into the pouch, along with oil and powders. In another drawer, he found a Colt revolver with an engraved plate sporting Oscar's name with a flourish etched beneath. He lobbed the Colt at Chester. His lanky companion caught it with ease.

"Oh Lawd! This jus' feels *right*." Chester waved the gun at Lena's blood-spattered face.

Eugene tied the sack and motioned for the front door.

Chester sprung to life. "Miss Lena, please 'scuse our abrupt exit. Don't wanna be rude and, ya' see, we'd love ta' chew the rag wit'chu, but we gotta hotfoot up to the Belle Fourche River." Chester toyed with Lena's collar, smearing a smattering of Oscar's blood around in a circle. "Now, thank ya' kindly for the clothes." He laughed. "We can't rightly be walking 'round in no stripes in public, now, can we?" He laughed and shook the pistol in her face. "And fer the guns, a'course. Eugene here's gonna go find him a pickaxe, ain't ya?" Chester smiled, his rotten teeth made Lena want to wretch. Eugene didn't respond. He was ransacking the place for useful supplies.

"Saw a couple of real fine horses out there. Gon' take them too. Oscar said we could." Chester couldn't contain his giggles. "We'll be on our way. An' don't you worry, I'm sure Eugene'll find 'at pickaxe 'fore too long."

Lena sobbed, caked in Oscar's blood. She could tell the wiry sadist felt no remorse about what he'd done to Oscar. Or to *her*.

"'Hell, at least he died fast," Chester offered flippantly as the duo made their way to the door. Near the threshold, Chester peered up at his gargantuan partner. "What you wanna do 'bout *her*?" Chester lowered his eyes and nudged a hunk of brain matter with his jailer's boot like a nervous child begging a parental favor. "'Cause, *well*, you got to do the feller. I 'magine it's only fair I get to do the *missus*."

Eugene smirked amenably. A toothy, rotten grin crept across Chester's gaunt face as he handed the Colt to his partner. "Here. Hang on to my gun, so I don't lose it. I ain't need it for her. I'm feelin'... *creative*." The connotations sounded sick, even to Eugene.

Lena let out a deafening shriek.

"Don't be long, Craven. Gonna be nightfall soon."

Chester dropped the handgun into Eugene's sack. "I won't, I promise! You have my word."

But Eugene Dempsey never trusted a thing Chester uttered. *There was no honor among thieves.*

The outlaw ducked to clear the frame and stepped outside.

"*Woooooo!*" Chester was overjoyed by the silent encouragement. He rubbed his hands together.

Eugene shut the wooden door behind him. He bent down and fished out the vital, folded paper from the pile of prisoner garb on the dusty ground. He stuffed it in the sack and headed toward the stables, strolling toward the stallions with long strides. His cider-tinted irises locked on his favorite of the bunch: an ebony Appaloosa with white dalmatian-spotted hindquarters.

A moment later, Lena's blood-curdling screams wafted out of the orifices of the house and echoed through the lonely, arid miles of Laramie ranch land.

CHAPTER FOUR

Prior to the early release on his own recognizance, Eugene had received clear instructions:

Follow the mountains. North a day-and-a-half to Buffalo, then east about a day to the Belle Fourche River. Then trace the body up a stretch.

Akecheta noted that, despite being tucked deep in the Black Hills, Eugene couldn't miss it.

They were miles past Buffalo now and Eugene scoured the flat, arid landscape for any semblance of the Bell Fourche up ahead. It had been days of trudging their tired horses along secretive mountain trails, battered by whipping winds, moving predominantly in the privacy of the night through mile-upon-mile of hungry western soil.

The duo trod for lengthy stretches with minimal breaks through dusty carrot-colored plains. The ground was like a dry tongue, dragging across the hooves of their hungry horses with every step.

Eugene had Chester in tow -- a slight addendum to the *original* plan -- but a welcome one as Chester would be a second set of eyes for the nightly lookout when they slept in shifts. More than that, Craven would be a second set of hands to help mine the trove and carry out the bounty of precious metals.

Eugene wasn't completely sure what he'd be capable of if he retrieved the fist-sized hunks of glimmering treasure promised by the old Native American between the bars of the Wyoming Territorial Prison, but he knew it would be enough to start over somewhere well East of this empty, lonely land. The sky was the limit. And what a vast, wide open sky it was.

Craven didn't know it but if it all went according to the big lug's plan, he'd be waking up in some seedy brothel in a few days with the tits of a haggard woman in one hand and a solitary hunk of gold in the other. A consolation prize for his help. Out of guilt. Out of respect. Eugene planned to be long gone with the rest of the loot. He didn't feel a pang of remorse for it either.

Chester would land on his feet. He was sure of it.

For an idiot who couldn't stifle his hyena's laugh to save his life, Chester had a coyote-like scrappiness about him. Back in prison, Eugene was baffled by his ability to manipulate guards with his quick wit and surprising charm. No one ever suspected it from the dumb string bean. He'd bounce gracefully from tactic to tactic until the right one clicked like a combination lock.

He can handle himself, Eugene thought. *He'll land on his feet.*

As the mustangs pattered on, thumping the hard soil with repetitious *clomps*, Eugene couldn't help but notice this was the most quiet Chester Craven had been in several years of shared involuntary confinement. Maybe the scrawny idiot was different when he was free; darker somehow, and far less playful.

Eugene could only *imagine* what he had done to the farmer's wife. Murder was fine, but any sort of depravity beyond that, including the sort of sickness that Craven exhibited, was not his style.

"Ya know…" Chester chugged from the stolen bottle of whiskey from Oscar's ranch, spilling tendrils down his sunken cheeks.

There it is, Eugene thought. *There goes the silence.*

"With my half a' the bounty, I might build me a big house down 'er in Arizona Territory. Hire me a buncha negro fellas fer' cheap and get it built right-quick. Then get me a good little woman," Chester droned on in a hopeful tone.

Eugene scoffed at the notion and stared ahead at the dusty stretch of plains. The wind whipped a sun-baked tumbleweed diagonally across their path. Eugene rumbled between gusts of wind and nodded in reference to the cheap liquor in Chester's hand. "Lay off that swill, now. Yer talkin' crazy."

"Oh, it speaks!" Chester jested. He offered up the bottle.

The sight of the bottle infuriated Eugene and reminded him of his partner's lack of focus on the task at hand. His smile faded as he thrashed the reins, sped up his horse and kicked the bottle violently from Craven's slender hand. The bottle flipped through the air and exploded loudly in a burst of shattered glass and booze, spooking Chester's flighty horse. The thirsty ground greedily soaked up the liquid.

"Why'd ya' do that?!" Chester fumed. He wanted to fight.

"We need ta' be sharp," Eugene growled. "You heard what the Lakota said! The Black Hills are littered with lawmen and Buffalo Soldiers. All of 'em gonna be looking for us, ya' *jiggy bonehead*! All of 'em know this here land better'n *both of us*."

"Why's you such an uppity *grind* all the time? You *ain't* better than me!" Chester was fed up with his partner's saltiness and pouted his gaunt face. He refused to make eye contact, which suited Eugene fine as he found Craven's moss-green eyes to be unnerving.

Chester's loud hick accent and erratic behavior struck Dempsey as a liability in broad daylight on the wide open plains, where sound carried miles on the whipping wind.

Popping one of the .44 caliber bullets from the lever-action shotgun he'd just acquired between Craven's platinum eyebrows seemed like a self-preserving move to quiet the fool. He reminded himself that he needed Chester to get in and out unscathed.

Eugene sucked in a deep drag of mountain air. Chester would soon be a memory and a shotgun blast would probably call more attention than the wild idiot's *mouth*.

"Soon you can buy all the nasty rotgut swill ya' want with your half." Eugene's voice boomed with absolution. His grimace was stern but secretly he sensed a tingle of joy inside.

He knew damn well Chester would never see half.

CHAPTER FIVE

Eugene smiled when Akecheta's directions proved to be spot-on. A wash of relief drifted over him as he spotted the flattened top of the giant butte mere miles in the distance. The colossal monolith stood before them, across the plains:

Bad God's Tower.

That's what the Lakota had called it.

The rushing current of the Bell Fourche was ice-cold despite the boiling sun simmering overhead. The heat was sweltering. The horses needed water and Chester desperately needed a bath. Eugene was sick of the pungent odor emanating from his greasy companion whipping past him every time the dry Wyoming winds blew, so he'd hurtled the spindly man in the river the moment they'd dismounted.

Now Chester sat on a rock, pouting like a petulant egg-white mongoose in his sopping, oversized farmer-duds. The sun had already started to drop and he feared the upcoming plunge in temperature.

Eugene carefully studied the amateur-squiggled circle punctuated with an "X" on his paper. Another wavy line was crudely sketched beside it, indicating the Bell Fourche, where they were now. The paper was a crude map, a gift from Akecheta illustrating a hidden passage -- allegedly loaded with unrefined gold -- leading into the base of *Bad God's Tower,* or as non-natives dubbed it:

Devil's Tower.

Eugene had heard stories about it while he pummeled spikes on the Northern Pacific, but he'd never laid eyes on it until now. He'd no clue how much gold the corridor contained, but imagined the haul would be worth all the trouble.

"Ya' owe me a pack 'a smokes when we get in to town." Chester fished a small box of soaked cigarettes and some matches out of his pocket, slapping them beside his damp six-shooter. Sun glinted off the barrel of the pistol.

Water dribbled down the rock's face and he examined a rust-colored symbol finger-painted on the side of it: A tribal depiction of a strange creature with two legs, a mouthful of craggy teeth, and an abnormal amount of blank eyes.

Chester dropped his oversized pants and shot a thick stream of canary-colored piss right at the middle of the design, turning his attention to the picturesque landscape as he emptied the rank contents of his bladder.

The magmatic rock butte loomed high in the wide-open cobalt sky over a thatch of pine trees. Oxidation of the land's iron infused the terrain with an artist's array of vibrancy. Rockfalls and devastating weather left snaggy cuts of raw squash-colored sandstone and stretches of maroon siltstone smeared along the face of the hills winding up to the extruded mass of volcanic material. Claw-like striations vertically striped the butte's face.

Eugene heard a Cheyenne legend in Montana years ago, on the railroad, alleging the tower's markings were caused by an 800-foot bear named *Mato* who tore at the tower trying to attack two children on the flattened summit.

Between them and the pines laid a plot of barren flatland overrun by playful prairie dogs. They'd have to be careful on the sparsely-grassed plains to keep the Appaloosas from snapping a leg in the frantically-burrowed dens. It wouldn't be wise to be stranded on foot in the Black Hills with such weighty and coveted bounty.

Eugene swept the loaded shotgun's single barrel across the flatland, eyeing the landscape through iron sights. He lowered the gun. Chester saw Eugene's calmness morph into uneasiness and he snatched up his six-shooter, ready for battle.

CHAPTER SIX

A half a mile upriver, the outlaws had been spotted. Walter Brown witnessed the escapees loading firearms from atop the jagged sedimentary rocks lining the distant riverbank.

Deep in his gut, Walter had hoped the absconders would stay far from the Northeastern corner of the Territory. Now the two detestable white men were on the doorstep of the land they, and the other dedicated members of the cavalry, had all sworn to protect.

Walter offered his binoculars to his trainee. After confirming the corporal's claim, George Fisher returned them. Walter popped the Civil War era kepi off his head and wiped the sweat from his dark skin with a sleeve, glancing at the yellow crossed sabers and the 9th cavalry designation before planting it back on his carob-tinted curls.

"Seems 'ese two raggedy jailbirds each got themselves a piece. Pistol an' a shotgun, single barrel, looks like." Walter put the binoculars back in his saddlebag and grabbed the reins of his onyx mustang.

"Got a plan, suh'?" George was ready for some excitement.

Walter spurred his mustang toward the fugitives. "Make sure 'dat carbine loaded, Fisha'."

"Whateva' you say, boss." George smiled.

CHAPTER SEVEN

Walter Brown watched blood ooze up from beneath the hole in his "*We Can: We Will*" Troop K patch stitched onto the bicep of his berry blue uniform. He didn't feel the searing pain in his upper arm yet. Only shock.

Things had gone south quickly.

"Private," Walter groaned into the open country air, "I'm hit!"

The blast from Chester's pistol firing echoed on the wind, blowing through the wind-swept meadow and bouncing its ringing tune off the siltstone surfaces.

The Buffalo Soldiers found themselves entrenched in a battle with two criminals that had little left to lose. *The most dangerous kind of man there is,* Walter thought.

Spooked by the resounding live fire, Chester's charcoal nag had long abandoned him. It was half a mile away now leaving him stranded behind a rock without any method of getaway. Eugene was smarter, as always. He'd tied his horse off around a riverside boulder after he'd forced Craven to take a *surprise* bath.

George galloped across the water's edge and immediately fired back a .45 caliber bullet from his rifle. He'd aimed at Chester Craven's sopping frame, missing the agile twig-of-a-man by centimeters, sending hunks of the sedimentary rock in front of the felon, hurtling explosively through the air like a meteor shower.

Eugene mounted his steed and heeled it hard. He thrashed the bridle and cantered across the prairie, leaving Craven to fend for himself.

Walter shook his reins and chased after the behemoth on the half-spotted Appaloosa. He locked eyes on Dempsey and snapped the stallion's reigns with force.

Chester slid a hand overhead and recovered his belongings from the rock, squishing them into his soaked pockets. *This was a hell of a time to be inebriated,* he thought. He popped his mossy, arresting eyes over the rock like a curious squirrel. Walter was chasing Eugene north, across the field, toward Devil's Tower. George, the other soldier, had overshot Chester's boulder and was stopped, reloading on horseback.

The rail-thin man stood, raised the gun in his damp right hand, struggling to hold his gun still. *Maybe Eugene was right about the booze,* he thought.

He fired a bullet right into the horse's head.

Bingo. Still got it.

The equine whipped, bucking George off, nearly crushing him beneath 600 pounds of floundering weight. As it whinnied violently, George tried to compose himself in the chaos. He searched frantically for his breech loader near the beast succumbing to its death throes. Chester fired again but Fisher dodged just in time, missing the bullet's trajectory by less than an inch.

After pulling the trigger, Chester took off like a drunken antelope toward the tower. By the time George Fisher retrieved the carbine from beneath his dying horse, Chester had a 40-yard lead on him. He followed in the rear, trampling through the dusty plains with the repeated thumping of his over-the-knee boots.

Eugene and the spotty Appaloosa made their way up to the rust-colored wall of siltstone. The horse's hooves pounded into the shale and powdery dirt as he traced the perimeter of the hill, looking for the first possible path to the higher level.

In the distance, a gunshot rang out again. This time, from George's Sharps carbine.

Eugene followed a narrow gravel trail uphill with reckless abandon. Walter continued past the path rife with jagged rocks, aware of a hill with a shallower grade that would take less of a toll on his steed. Having been stationed in the Black Hills for over three years, Walter knew this land better than he knew himself.

To Eugene, however, it was all wild, treacherous new country.

Dempsey's equine skidded clumsily onto the craggy landing that created the pedestal of the towering volcanic extrusion. Despite his divided attention, he was awe-struck at the monumental size of it up close. Nearly 1,000 feet of extruded hexagonal columns loomed overhead. Fallen chunks of long-cooled magma-shards were scattered around the base like an igneous moat, shattered into fragments by the bell-like foundation of the butte.

Walter slowed within a decent range of the fugitive and awkwardly yanked the Colt Army .45 caliber pistol out of his side holster with his left hand. His horse stirred beneath him. Intense pain surged through him now that the shock had worn off. He was a terrible shot with his left hand, but thanks to the cartridge lodged in his right bicep, he had no choice.

"It don't have ta' be like this, Dempsey," Walter yelled. He didn't want to kill Eugene, but the outlaw left him little choice. He felt a knot in his stomach, tightening like the rope on a rodeo calf's neck.

Eugene dropped the reins, yanked his shotgun over his shoulder, cocked the lever and fired. The bullet hit, blasting Walter in the right arm, again, inches above the first injury. The force surged him backward, end-over-end and into a crevice between two jagged boulders.

The obscured corporal screamed out in devastating agony. He rallied himself and fired back at Eugene immediately.

Missed.

The sound of the gun spooked the Appaloosa. It bucked powerfully, tossing Eugene's enormous body like a rag doll into the crags, slamming against the unforgiving metal of his shotgun barrel. The saddlebags and the burlap sack rained down on him, nearly impaling him with the point of the exposed pickaxe.

His horse took off.

Sweat pouring down his ebony skin, Walter discharged again, exploding a hunk out of the saddlebag in Eugene's hand. Eugene dropped the pack, turned, and cocked the lever again. He fired another blast at the soldier, missing him by a sizable distance.

The fall from the horse had rocked Dempsey. His spent shell casing flung out into the rubble. Eugene roared with rage. He clutched a boulder to steady himself and noticed blood smeared across the face of the rock.

Dried blood.

Confused, Eugene dashed away from the bloody rock toward a thatch of pine trees that would provide some cover.

Hollering a pained war cry, Walter fired at Dempsey twice more, missing both. *His aim was shit with his left hand.*

Another shot rang out, further down. It was George. Chester dove into a pile of dried brush at the bottom of the hill. George reloaded and then blasted at Chester again.

"Careful, private!" Walter screamed out, slumped and bleeding between two rocks and hissing in agony. "Dempsey's in da' trees!"

Illuminated by the tobacco-colored sunset hanging in the expansive sky, Eugene saw colorful religious offerings of swaddled cloth near the tower's walls, no doubt placed there by native tribes. But Eugene was infatuated by the bizarre sound seemingly excreting from the rock wall behind the gifts.

Muffled screeches.

Eugene and Walter both heard dampened shrieks emanating from the earth. The convict crept to a closer tree as stealthily as his gigantic, imposing frame would allow. Using the pickaxe to pull himself up, he climbed up the angular stones, cursing the farmer's ill-fitting boots and the raw blisters that made every step searingly painful. He listened intently for more of the dull screams, but they had fallen silent.

Where was the entrance he'd seen on the Lakota's map?

It should have been straight ahead, but all he saw was a mess of fallen stony rubble.

Was he on the wrong side? Had he lost track of the river?

Walter watched Eugene from a gap between two huge boulders, squinting over the iron sight of his trusty cavalry rifle. With his shaking left hand he opened the action and loaded a linen-wrapped cartridge. He slammed it closed and cocked the hammer, popped a primer pellet in the hole and lined up his shot. He followed the grinding of the rusty pick across stone, carefully poised on the trigger.

Beyond the axe, another smothered screech oozed from beneath the rocks stopping Eugene cold. A chill rushed over him.

"Psst!"

The whispering sound came from behind, sending Walter into a full-body sweat. The wounded corporal craned his dark-complected face around in time to see the toe of Chester's stolen cowboy boot as it smashed mercilessly into his **eye**. The force thrust him against the rocks and fired the still-forward-facing rifle, **narrowly** missing Eugene's head, and rupturing shards out of the hardened magma behind **the felon.**

Crunching rocks crackled through the landscape and Eugene instinctively peered up at the origin. Vibrations from the guns had started a rock slide of gigantic proportions. The outlaw hurled his massive body away from the tower, toward the other men, and narrowly escaped the path of a colossal, falling hunk of rock.

Frenzied screeches grew louder beneath the growing pile as more chunks rained down, as if thrown by some infuriated deity above. Overhead, the hexagonal striations crumbled further, unloading enormous fragments from the sky, like frogs in a biblical plague.

Bad God's Tower.

The name made sense now.

The explosive force of the rockslide rattled the ground. The rubble beneath them tumbled down the tree-peppered hill, opening up what appeared to be a narrow, darkened entrance into the tower's base.

"Eugene!" Chester pointed out the ingress below a waterfall **of crackling stone shards.**

But he'd already noticed it.

They all had.

Awe-stricken by the existence of the hidden passageway the destruction had just unearthed, Chester maneuvered his agile body to dodge the rain of rock. George sprung up after him, determined to stop the evasive criminal at any cost. He fired his rifle into Chester's left kneecap, ripping a hole through the spindly man's bone and cartilage, and dropping him hard on the rock pile. Overhead, magmatic chunks ripped from the columns of the tower, exploding in bursts around Chester like detonated grenades.

The cascade slowed to nuggets and dust. Chester wailed in agonizing pain, crawling into the hollow. Not far behind, Eugene lunged toward the entrance while George and Walter reloaded.

His hulking figure reached the narrow mouth and a claustrophobic sea of horror sloshed through him like icy ocean waves. It was a tight fit, snaking down like a giant mole tunnel into blackened, unknown depths.

BOOM!

Another shot rang out, hitting Eugene square in the hand, launching his pickaxe into the rubble. He roared, clutched his gnarled, bleeding palm to his chest and retrieved the axe with the unharmed fist.

Damn it, Walter cursed himself silently. He'd been aiming for Eugene's torso. He reloaded on adrenaline and muscle memory as George leapt over some rocks at the men.

"C'mon, Eugene!" Chester waved his blood-soaked hand, beckoning him into the tight subterranean passage. Eugene wasn't just scared, he was petrified. He wondered for a moment if going back to prison would be less of a punishment than suffocating to death in an enclosed underground burrow.

Chester threw himself down the striated slide head-first and growled at the pain surging through him every time his shattered knee touched the surface. Gravity tugged him down into the unknown.

George hurtled toward the cavern.

"Halt, private!" Walter shouted in protest, short of breath. "'At tunnel don't lead nowhea' but trouble. Guard the entrance!"

CHAPTER EIGHT

Inside, the tunnel narrowed around Chester's thin frame and Eugene hollered out, close behind. Eugene chose a feet-first approach. He couldn't stomach the idea of sliding head-first into God-knows-what.

He tried to soothe himself by remembering what the Lakota said about the fist-sized hunks of pure gold hidden in the base of Bad God's Tower, and how it was enough to make a hundred men rich beyond their wildest dreams. Eugene remembered a guard talking about how Akecheta had been convicted up north with enough greenbacks to build another prison from scratch, which only added to the legitimacy of the tall tales.

Eugene felt his hulking body jam tight in the cramped tunnel. His lungs had compressed with the confining pressure. He couldn't seem to get enough air.

Hyperventilating, he jiggled the pick overhead into the existing grooves in a futile attempt to move himself in either direction. The long gouges in the magma made it seem like giant animals had clawed the passage into existence, tearing giant fissures as it dug into the deep. Or maybe the scratches were from the pickaxes of others, long before this horrid day. Eugene wondered if perhaps the goldmine had already been plundered.

Maybe this was all for naught.

Eugene knew if he could expel a deep breath and hold it, he might have the extra inch or two needed to wiggle his packed body downward.

Below his feet, Chester birthed himself out of the rodent-like tunnel leaving a wet smear of blood from his leg on the gouged black floor of the tight volcanic stone slide.

He found himself in absolute darkness.

He leaned against a wall, plucking the damp pack of matches from his bloody pants. He struck one against the box repeatedly until it caught fire. Limping forward, he dimly illuminated his surroundings.

"Eugene!"

Chester's hyena-like laughter resonating up through the tunnel brought Dempsey no comfort. He no longer hid the panic in his voice.

"Chester, for the love 'a God, *help*!"

"Eugene, you gotta see 'is!" Chester giggled, hobbling toward a huge wall of clustered gold. "I'll be dipped!" He doubled over to laugh and buckled from the injury to his knee. He winced through enormous pain. A perfect gait was a minuscule price to pay for the vast riches before him.

Chester heard a noise. The sound of rock-on-rock. Something was grinding in the depths beyond the gold.

"Help me, you idiot!" Eugene screamed, panicked, cutting Chester's investigation short.

As the flame died out, Chester tossed the match and felt his way back through the pitch-black enclosure. He threaded his stringy body into the tunnel and squirmed diagonally up until he felt Eugene's stolen cowboy boots smacking the sides in terrified, staccato movements.

"Stop kickin'!" He grabbed Eugene's thick calf and wrenched it hard.

Trapped in the clawed, oppressive passage, a nerve-shattering thought entered Eugene's mind: At some point, he'd have to get *out* of here, which probably meant traveling back through this tubal hell.

Chester yanked the perspiring outlaw hard and Eugene slid toward him. Eugene gasped a relieved breath as his chest dislodged from the narrows. Chester crawled back into the darkness, careful not to put pressure on his knee, and both wriggled out into the onyx void.

Freedom.

"This place stinks." Eugene gasped putrid air and clutched his pickaxe as if the splintered handle offered some solace. "It's rank! Smell' like somethin' crawled in here an' died."

As the words left Eugene's deformed lips, he hoped that the same fate would not be true about him. After all, he had no idea how he was going to get *out* of this noxious pit, especially without the aid of gravity. He imagined stuffing himself back into the burrow to escape, packed like a ball in a cannon. He shuddered.

"We gon' be *rich*, Eugene! " Chester struck another match.

This time, the light illuminated something unexpected.

Something *living*.

A lurking biped with a cluster of foggy crimson eyes swiveled its long neck down at Eugene's face. As a nearly seven-foot-tall man, Dempsey had never been dwarfed by anything. *Until now.*

"What... the..." Chester's jaw dropped as they stared up at the albino creature. Glossed pale skin was pulled taut over a bizarre skeletal system. Four wretched arm-like appendages jutted from what they assumed was the being's torso.

The match died, swallowing them in pure darkness.

Chester's shaking hand rattled the tiny box of matches. He struck another and terror surged through the chests of both grown men.

Just as they feared, *they hadn't imagined it.*

The melanin-devoid being sniffed Chester with deep-set nostrils torn deep into its gluey face. It spread the slick flesh of its lips, contorting its orifice into a strange expression of pleasure. The slow grin revealed a horrific mass of hundreds of needle-like teeth. The syringe-like set of gnashers seated together perfectly and had geometric spacing akin to seeds on a dandelion blow-ball. Each two-inch tooth dripped with viscous slime that had the stench of noxious poison.

A vertebral row of flesh-webbed spikes flicked up like the dorsal spines of a lionfish. Long, bony extrusions peeled out from both sides of its body. Foot-long stony nails curled out of every digit of each of the organism's bizarre hands. It lumbered closer and another beast, just like the first, edged in from the darkened cavity beyond the gold.

Eugene raised the pickaxe with his right hand. His left was still bleeding and tender and his limp ring-finger was only held on by a thread. The nerves felt like searing fire every time he flexed it.

He recalled the foreboding look on Akecheta's face when attempting to unlock his cell door and the scarred indentations on the Lakota's gnarled hands. Had he *seen* these beasts and lived to tell the tale? Suddenly, the old man's desire to stay imprisoned didn't seem so foolish after all. Eugene now also had a surprising longing for the safety of the Wyoming Territorial Prison -- and its protective iron bars.

At least in there, he *was the monster...*

A third fog-eyed beast blindly slunk out from behind the golden mound, dividing their attention. The third, shorter by a foot, lanced its long stone fingers rapidly into the igneous rock beside itself. It repeated with the impaling digits on its other three extremities, dragging its diabolical feet limply upward through the air. It skittered until perched, bat-like, overhead.

Too terrified to run once the match burned out, Eugene whispered. The quiver in his voice begged for another lit stick. "Still got any bullets in the Colt?"

"*Probably three*." Chester swallowed hard and struggled to light another damp match. His hands scrambled in the darkness.

Three would be enough. It had to be.

Blinded by darkness, Eugene heard rustling and whipped his head, following the sound. He could only listen for their new locations, clutching the pickaxe. One of the beasts scampered overhead. A wet, acidic trail of spit dribbled onto his curly mop of hair, burning into his scalp. He swung the pick awkwardly upward, missing completely and burying the point in the overhang above, showering both men with pebbles and sediment.

Another match snapped in Chester's hands. "Why'd ya have to throw me in the goddamn *Belle Fourche*?!"

Eugene regretted it now, but nowhere near as much as he regretted coming down here.

The creatures emitted throaty gurgling noises, a primitive form of their species' ability to echo-locate prey. Their grotesque babbling swelled, then abruptly stopped, leaving the duo in utter silence.

In the struggle to light another, Chester dropped the box of remaining matchsticks, scattering them around the dusty stone floor. Eugene's heart sank at the sound.

Chester retrieved one and cocked the farmer's Colt .45. He dragged the match face across the abrasive engraving on the pistol's grip. It lit up with a harsh *chhhh,* the sound echoing off the clawed walls.

On terrified instinct, Chester fired dead ahead where the torso of the first beast had been. Stone exploded. The bullet ricocheted off several hardened surfaces, retiring in the darkness somewhere beyond.

The beast was no longer there and the gunfire sent them clacking and cavorting around the rocks. As the beings screeched on, the outlaws sensed they were far outnumbered. The clatter alluded there were exponentially more than just three of those... *things*.

Despite hearing them clearly, none of the beasts were within the small orb of light cast by the lone match. The venomous spittle on Eugene's head was actively burning through his singeing scalp, dissolving a patch of thick, greasy hair.

The men glanced up. Two of the creatures dangled tenuously above them with their spindly, granitic talons picked into deep-bored holes in the ceiling. A third, behind Chester, sunk its mouth full of needly teeth into the back of his neck with terrifying force. Chester yelped as the beast began to gnaw and crunch its way through the back of his skull, slurping up the gush of blood pouring from the head wound with a rubbery, slime-coated, flapping tongue. It slapped like a sticky wad of lower intestine, the fluid burning everywhere it made contact.

Eugene swung and buried his pickaxe into its spiny shoulder blade. Without letting go of Chester's head, the beast used both right extremities to slap Eugene away and, in tandem, removed the rusted implement, hurtling the heavy pick across the cave.

Chester screamed.

Unarmed now, another dangling beast wrapped a fistful of curled nails around Eugene's throat and whipped the broad outlaw off the ground. Through black nothingness, Eugene choked out, *"Chester, shoot!"*

Terrorized and losing consciousness, Chester had almost forgotten he had a gun. In fact, he'd almost forgotten *everything he'd ever known.* The creature slurped brain matter through an acid-bored hole in his skull. Chester grew weak, his mind barely grasping consciousness.

Chester aimed blindly behind himself in the darkness and fired, hoping it was the right trajectory to hit the beast.

It wasn't.

He missed. The thundering sound of the colt quaked the walls and sent the garish critters clacking around in hysteria.

Life began to vacate Chester's body as fast as his brain tissue, and with what little of his life-force remained, he remembered the rust-red drawing on the river rocks. How was he to know the crude finger painting -- probably drawn in *blood* -- was a warning of nightmarish albino beasts?

We never should've come here. That was the last thought Chester had.

His body went limp in its claws and the beast sank its stony nails deeper into his chest, puncturing his lungs like spongy balloons. Eugene heard the air seep from his partner's dying carcass followed by the thump of his thin frame as it was hurled, with inhuman strength, across the cavern.

The fog-eyed beast clutched Eugene from the ceiling, piercing its thumbnails into his shoulders and throat as he struggled to free himself. The weight of his imposing body finally tugged through the beast's grasp and Eugene *thwacked* against the wet floor, bathed in Chester's freshly-spilled blood.

He felt around the blackness for anything of use, listening intently over his quick gasps for air. His gigantic palms grazed the spilled matches and box, now soaked in hot, viscous liquid.

Yes!

He tried to strike one of the drenched sticks on the floor. It snapped between his bloody fingers. He wiped one on his ill-fitting pants to dry it off and scratched it against the prickly stubble of his jawline -- a trick he'd learned on the railroad. It hurt like hell but it struck, dimly illuminating the wet, ruby-streaked path in front of him.

Chester's still, sinewy body draped over another protruding mountain of raw gold, his unsettling moss-green eyes stuck open wide and horrified. The reeking funk was overpowering. Eugene clasped a bloody hand over his nose and mouth and stepped beyond to examine the source of the wafting stench behind Craven's body:

A decomposing tangle of butchered men. An orgy of death and greed gnarled like the roots of a tree together in a heaped mass. The explorers formed a liquefied mound of rotting tissue, clothes, and bones.

Spoiling organs, thick with larvae, sat piled in a lumpy mess of flesh. Feasting flies and hungry maggots writhed and squirmed, giving the festering mass of death its own sort of undulating life.

Eugene couldn't stop staring at the pile of eviscerated humans -- humans that had trekked in with the same rapacity in their hearts. Eugene could almost smell the putrid scent of avarice wafting up through the decaying human muck.

Dear God, I'm never leaving this place. Eugene felt its certainty in his thumping heart.

"Come out, both'a ya!" Walter's voice bellowed down the darkened hole behind him. The soldier's calm tone meant he had no idea what kind of horrors they'd experienced in the cavern, from just feet away.

"Help me!" From the cave floor, Eugene's cry was childlike, like a runaway who realized how brutal the world really was and just wanted to come home. "It's just me down here. *Chester…* Chester is…" Unable to say the words, Eugene cried hard, spit trailing from his gaping maw, frozen in a silent scream. It was the first time *real* tears had escaped his eyes in decades. Though he'd planned to double-cross the man, he still cared about the sadistic coot. Chester had been his only friend.

"Put ya' guns down and come on out. 'Is all gon' be alright." Walter cooed in an attempt to deescalate the situation.

The gun!

In the chaos, Eugene had forgotten about Chester's Colt. He struck another match and scrounged the ground searching for Chester's pistol with his lacerated hand.

By the time he laid a hand on it, several more creatures had amassed above him. There was now an army of long-nailed beasts clutched to the ceiling, dribbling long stalagmite-like strings of rank spit from their chilling, toothy grins.

They were *all* smiling.

Every one of them.

He eyed the revolver's chamber. Chester was wrong.

One bullet left.

Eugene remembered their violent reactions to the gun blasts, no doubt due to their sensitive hearing and existence in solitude. If he could just get them away from the mouth of the tunnel, he could try to weasel back out. Or maybe he could scare them out.

The cluster stared, waiting to strike. He moved toward the mouth of the slide and they followed him, picking slowly into closer holes. He aimed at the nearest in the mass and fired off one final ear-splitting shot, ripping a hole in its chest. It plummeted and whirled, pained, on the floor, slapping its slimy tongue around and emitting a guttural, deafening scream.

The others clamored and ricocheted in a mobbed panic, trampling each other like giant bats through the tunnel, crawling haphazardly out almost as a single, heaving mass. The conjoined fleshy litter of bony, albino, multi-eyed creatures evacuated the canal in unison.

The eclipsed hole opened up as the last creature escaped and Eugene could hear them clawing up the face of Devil's Tower. A thin beam of the sky's light flitted across the scratched tunnel walls.

It has to be now, he thought. *Before they come back!*

Before more could appear from the deeper bowels of the cave.

God only knows how many exist.

Eugene took a panicked breath, dove in like a swimmer, arms overhead, and packed himself into the hole. He began to wriggle upward, which was much slower than going down.

From fifteen feet above him, he heard the terrified Buffalo Soldiers open fire with their cavalry rifles.

"What 'da *hell* is 'dat?!" It was Walter's voice.

BOOM!

Deep vibrations rippled through Eugene as the tunnel swallowed him, constricting his breath like a boa. Panic clamped down. He saw purple sky beyond his disfigured hand, caked in blood and decomposing gold-miner sludge. Unable to advance his shoulders further, anxiety overtook him.

No one could hear his screams over the thunderous gun blasts beyond.

BOOM!

Another resounding shot was followed by quaking tremors in the earth and the surrounding rock. He couldn't move at all now. Dempsey was completely stuck, jammed tightly in the tunnel unable to kick, unable to flail...

Unable to *breathe*...

CHAPTER NINE

OOM!

The blast rattled the earth beneath their knee-high boots. Walter stared upward at the behemoth hunk of striated rock, transfixed as the flock of translucent egg-white creatures skittered up the grooved face of the stone wall. They clamored toward the butte atop the landmark like nothing he had ever seen before. He stared from between the modicum of safety the two boulders offered, mouth gaping in awe and terror.

For those moments, he forgot about the surging pain of his bullet wound. He forgot about his wife, his past, his struggles. He needed to rally all of his mental energy to wrap his mind around the terrifying sight of what had just squeezed out of that narrow canal of rocky earth.

His left hand trembling, he slammed open the action and pulled out his final linen-swaddled cartridge. The man's pockets and satchel were empty. Ammo wasn't abundant and the buffalo soldiers had to disperse what they had among themselves.

"You got any more?" The Corporal asked, holding up the projectile.

"No 'suh." George's voice wavered, his tone drenched in fear. "This my last one." The stark whites of the young soldier's bulging eyes peered past the bill of his kepi, drifting up toward the scratching beasts clawing their way skyward, scaling the tower.

A tendril of sweat dribbled down the smooth side of his face. Walter had almost mistaken it for a tear.

"If Eugene wants his freedom this bad, he can have it, 'far as I'm concerned."

Walter nodded at the boy, wise beyond his years. "Is' like poker, son. Sometimes you gotta fold a bad hand."

He felt like a coward for letting the words escape his dry lips, chapped from the battering Wyoming gusts along this dehydrated stretch of plains. The same ones he took an oath to protect.

George glanced over, managing a breathy laugh. "This most definitely a bad hand. This hand here… this too rich for my blood."

Walter forced a pained chuckle. Time to retreat. "We need backup. This here, this a suicide mission." He cocked his weapon, pressed his last primer pellet inside, and closed it cautiously, so as not to jostle his injured shoulder more than he had to.

"Let's git," he mumbled.

One of the creatures screeched above them, rammed by the thrashing head of its larger brethren. The first skidded down the tower's face, scrambling to grasp its stony talons into the grooves. They wouldn't catch. It tumbled down toward the buffalo soldiers with an echoing pterodactyl-like scream, smacking onto the rock mound at the base near them in a tangle of strange, knobby limbs. Pebbles exploded, showering the soldiers. Sharp spines and abnormal bones covered with taut, thin tissue clattered about, righting itself on two hideous hind legs.

George screamed, a reflexive reaction to the sheer proximity of the beast and fired his last shot right into the papery, colorless skin of the demon's face.

The percussive force ripped the meat away like tattered fabric exposing its anomalous skeletal system. The hole in its toothy face dripped with gore and crimson ichor, splattering to the clinking jumble of rocks and Indian offerings in clumpy disarray below its multiple extremities. It's partially detached jaw, riddled with hundreds of white toothpick fangs, hung limply from its skull. The creature hunkered down, narrowing its foggy, lifeless blind eyes and listening for the men as it crept closer to the source of the blast.

It hobbled toward them. The soldiers stopped breathing with the sudden understanding that the *thing* with the evil, blank stare was trying to echo-locate them.

George struggled to stand, whipping his head in circles to try to find the fastest way off the rock pile. The gravel below him gurgled beneath his weight, giving his location away.

The savage creature snapped its neck, the bones popping, slack mandible swinging, it aimed what remained of its impossibly mangled face right at him.

Walter fired his last shot.

BOOM!

CHAPTER TEN

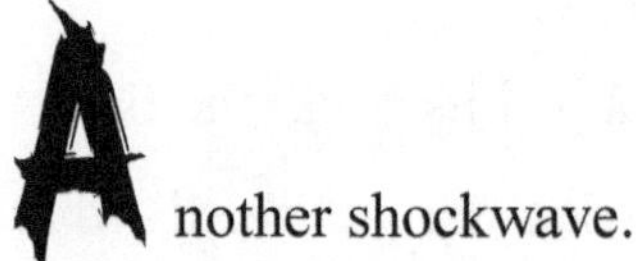nother shockwave.

"Jesus!" The voice outside the cave erupted as a cry.

Rocks cracked above Eugene. He heard pieces of the tower breaking loose. His small, strangled shouts for help only echoed back into his own face. He wriggled like a wild trout, making no headway.

"George! Oh, God! George!" Eugene heard another voice cry out, like a mourning father clutching his dying son. "Please God!"

The pleading morphed into screaming. The sound trailed further away from his stony coffin now and Eugene felt true terror.

The voice was fleeing. *They were abandoning him.*

Eugene's drooling, gut-wrenching screams for help were stifled by the crashing tumble of rock columns slicing against the face of Devil's Tower.

Bad God's Tower, indeed.

The outlaw's heart nearly stopped when the last beam of dusky light was snuffed out, leaving him compressed and entombed in utter darkness. He yelled again, the lack of oxygen like inebriation in his brain.

No one could hear him now.

As Eugene struggled and thrashed in the striated coffin of cooled volcanic rock, he thought about how, for years, he swore to a green-eyed psychopath he'd die a free man.

Yet, during his final, panicked, constricted breaths in the now-concealed tunnel of *Bad God's Tower*, Eugene Dempsey thought about the irony…

Who was the prisoner now?

ABOUT THE AUTHOR

Erica Summers is an independent filmmaker, writer, film industry grip, and artist with an unwavering passion for horror. Several of her award-winning feature films have screened worldwide including Obsidian, Mister White, & Loverboy (on Amazon Prime and most streaming services.) Though born and raised in Wyoming, Erica spent most of her life in the swampy American South. She now resides in Connecticut where she works in film and writes horror fiction. In her downtime, the bizarre, bisexual, cancer-survivor is typically slathered in garden dirt, fishing, or devouring horror movies with her boyfriend and two jack russell *terrors*.

Recent publications include, "The Mother" (*Their Ghoulish Reputation* by Dark Lake Publishing*)*, "Tines" (Eerie River Publishing's *It Calls From Below)*, "*Painted in Vermilion*" *(*Eerie River Publishing's *Air: Elemental Series)*, "*All the Same Color on the Inside*" *(*Black Hare Press' *Year Five Anthology)*, "*Take a Breath*" *(*HellBound Books' *Anthology of Splatterpunk,)* as well as her novel, "*Mantis*" (on Amazon & Godless,) and two novellas, "Bad God's Tower" and "Obsidian."

ACKNOWLEDGEMENTS

I just want to say a quick thank you to a few people who made this possible:

--Heather Wohl, my sister, my best friend, my hero, and the first eyes on any project of mine, this woman is one of the best humans in existence. She's a horror and fantasy writer too and you should definitely keep your eyes peeled for her upcoming releases.

--Amanda Jean Ruzsa, my editor, who did the final pass of polish on this fun western romp. She is worth her weight in gold. And Mark Anthony, my proofreader who helped catch so many things before I even sent it to Amanda.

--My ARC team including Ash Ericmore, Steve Stred Otis Bateman (Travis Davis), John Ryland, Chisto Healy, Mia Faller, as well as the awesome indie reviewers who read advanced copies like Corrina Morse, Brendon James, Leeanne Wright, etc, etc. Thank you all so much. I appreciate the work you all put into this.

--And more than anything, thank YOU, readers. Without you, this would mean nothing.

FIRST CHAPTER SNEAK PEEK

OF

VANITY KILLS

(Available in Ebook, Paperback, & Hardcover 9/1/23)

ONE

The menacing smell of death hangs thick in the air, hovering like a dense cloud of relentless mosquitoes in the hot July humidity. The hazy Louisiana sky looms vibrant and ominous overhead, as though colored by the blessed smoke of a voodoo shaman.

There is fire. Licking its forked, heathen tongue up the side of an oak tree. Glittering in the squares of shattered glass, scattered among crunchy detritus and powdered dirt. The fractals reflect a million copies of the harrowing scene around them like millions of microscopic television sets. There's a spray of pieces on the seat, dispersed unevenly in coagulating blood like clustered diamond flecks around leaky garnet stones.

Dark smoke billows from the sputtering engine of the silver SUV, belching thick, steamy plumes of blackened poison into the air, blooming out from beneath the crumpled hood.

The area is unusually silent beyond the mechanical hisses and whirs of the once-growling engine. Deafening even, in the absence of the typical southern wilderness cacophony. The birds and locusts gawk silently at the tragedy, watching the sudden stillness of it all as reverent onlookers.

A horrific scream rips the air, reverberating like a megaphone off the miles of bone-straight pavement ahead. It's guttural, like something almost inhuman but decidedly male.

The river of glass tinkles as his lacerated hands tremble their way across the seat. His eyes strain to focus. Fear sits thick in his gasping throat. A blood-smeared airbag is deployed over him like a burst bubble of gleaming white chewing gum, claustrophobically suffocating him with draped fabric. It's deflated over the bulge in his lap, like a cloth doorway to the fresh hell and years of nightmares that lie beneath. He weakly touches it, hands tremoring in utter shock.

His trembling fingers tangle in the lock of wet, dark hair beneath the folds of the spattered material. It's all become partly detached from the crushed human skull pinned between the bent steering column and his lap.

Her *skull.*

There's no one else's it could be, though he prayed to God that he was somehow wrong.

Please *God* let it be wrong.

The fleeting moments before the crash rush back like a boulder rolling downhill.

Picking up speed.

Smacking him in the face like a Mack truck.

He screams again, leaving every trace of his soul in the cry as it dissipates into the muggy ether above the burgeoning eddy of gray smoke.

Pink spit dribbles down his gashed face and neck, scored with straight cuts from the exploded windshield. He writhes, unable to free his pinned lower half from the nightmare he's opened his eyes to.

The miserable nightmare he'd do anything to wake from.

But he didn't understand misery yet.

No, that *he would learn in the cruel years to come because in this moment, he cannot even begin to fathom the fallout and repercussions of one single moment of time.*

Lives altered forever from one careless over-correction.

He screams so loud again that he chokes on a lungful of smoke, hacking up pink drool, sucking in snot and tears. He coughs again until he gags out the window, where he locks eyes with a panting dog.

He swears the mutt has a judgemental look in his eyes. And why shouldn't it? It's seen everything.

It scrutinizes him, the spotted catahoula pup. Raising its young, curious face at the wreckage with its paws crossed, lounging calmly on its belly in the grass.

As if he had no part in this.

As if, for him, *everything will be just fine.*

As if, for him, *the world is* not *on fire.*

***

MORE HORRORS FROM ERICA SUMMERS

Mantis: A Novel

SYNOPSIS: How far would you go to stop a biblical travesty? Out of nowhere, Mantis, a chain-smoking bisexual with no filter, finds herself in the midst of a demon apocalypse. She recruits a reformed prostitute, bubbly stripper, and hopelessly-romantic tag-along to try to stop Revelations in its tracks. Will the lovable degenerates save mankind? Locked-and-loaded with sinister creatures, violent action, twisted villains, and a heroine who has all the charm of a rabid wolverine. Mantis will take you on a wild adventure through the bowels of the American South and drop you on the doorstep of the Devil. Mantis is a blood-soaked horror-comedy full of guts, gore, and good times.

Available February 6, 2024

Writhe: A Novella

By Erica Summers & H. M. Wohl

SYNOPSIS: Garrett was a normal New Yorker, appeasing annoying neighbors and paying over-inflated rent for a dumpy little 4th-story apartment in Hell's Kitchen… Until the *larvae* hatched.

As Garrett unleashes his violent wrath upon the unsuspecting city of Manhattan, NYPD'S-own mismatched duo, Luca Triton and Mel Trido, are on a tense mission to find the lunatic behind the rampage before he can murder again.Before the Times Square ball drops, will they capture the homicidal madman in a surging sea of potential victims?

Available February 27, 2024

The Rictus Grin & Other Tales of Insanity

A Collection of Short Stories

By Erica Summers

Available May 28, 2024

Obsidian (Feature Film)

The independent feature film version of *Vanity Kills.* (Available on most streaming services)

Mister White (Feature Film)

FILM SYNOPSIS: After a rowdy gang of friends viciously target quiet newcomer, Tyler Rooney, the bullied teen seeks deadly revenge in the form of a hoodoo-conjured demon named Mister White.

(Available on most streaming services including Prime)